Mim, Gym, and June

www.houghtonmifflinbooks.com

The text of this book is set in Gills Sans.
The illustrations are gouache.

Library of Congress Cataloging-in-Publication Data

Roche, Denis.
Mim, gym, and June / written and illustrated by Denis Roche.
p. cm.
Summary: When the second grade starts to take gym class with the third-graders,
Mim finds herself intimidated by the larger June.
ISBN 0-618-15254-7 (hardcover)
[1. Bullies—Fiction. 2. Schools—Fiction.] I. Title.
PZ7.R5843 Mi 2003
[Fic]—dc21
2002005092

Printed in Singapore
TWP 10 9 8 7 6 5 4 3 2 1

To Oliver and Clara,
first-est together

Mim, Gym, and June

Written and illustrated by
Denis Roche

 Houghton Mifflin Company Boston 2003

Mim was small for her age.
She needed a stool to reach the sink.
Her hands weren't big enough to open the peanut butter jar.
She sat on her knees to see better in the auditorium.

Mim didn't mind being small.
She fit into the best hiding places.
The lunch ladies gave her extra grilled cheese sandwiches.
The busy principal always remembered her name.

For Mim, the absolute best thing about being small was that she always got to be first in her second grade line.

One Monday morning, Mim's teacher made an announcement.
   "From now on, you'll have gym with the third-graders," she said.
When it was time, Mim's class followed Coach Beeker down the hall.
As usual, Mim was first.

The third-graders were lined up and waiting.

"Move it, shorty!" growled a voice above Mim.

Mim looked up. June, the biggest third-grader, was sneering down at her.

"You're in my place," snarled June. "*I'm* always first."

"Oh, dear!" said June's teacher. "In the third grade we line up biggest to smallest."

"No matter," said Coach Beeker, pointing to a spot. "June can be first starting from here."

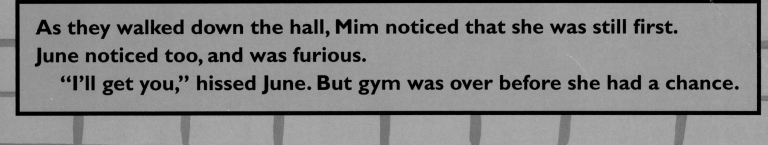

As they walked down the hall, Mim noticed that she was still first.
June noticed too, and was furious.

"I'll get you," hissed June. But gym was over before she had a chance.

The second and third-graders wouldn't have gym again until Friday.
Mim knew June was growing angrier and angrier.

On Tuesday, June cut the lunch line in front of Mim and gulped down
the rest of the grilled cheese sandwiches.

"I'll devour you too!" she said, and gnashed her teeth.

On Wednesday, she stuck her head over the bathroom stall and made faces at Mim.

"Just you wait!" she threatened.

On Thursday, she hogged the monkey bars.
"Gym tomorrow!" she roared from the top. "I'll get you then, Mim!"

That night Mim got a stomachache thinking of gym and June.

"She's enormous!" she said, sniffing.

"Third-graders aren't that big," said Mim's mother. "Maybe you can do something to be friends."

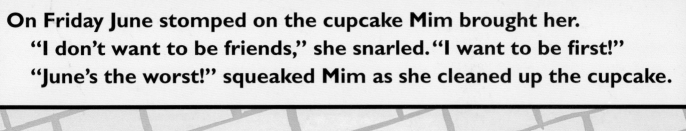

On Friday June stomped on the cupcake Mim brought her.
"I don't want to be friends," she snarled. "I want to be first!"
"June's the worst!" squeaked Mim as she cleaned up the cupcake.

The second-graders made up a song and quietly sang it all the way to the gym.

> "Mim's the first-est,
> June's the worst-est,
> Mim's still the first-est,
> So hah, hah, hah."

June heard the song, and by the time the second and third-graders got to the gym, she was ripping mad. Her face was red and her hair stood on end.

Coach Beeker sat everyone in a circle around the mat.

"Gym Olympics today," he said. "We'll start with wrestling, then running, and finally an obstacle course."
June cracked her knuckles with glee.

"I'll wrestle first!" she volunteered, and Mim's whiskers curled with fear.

One by one, June wrestled the second and third-graders. She easily beat everyone, and soon it was Mim's turn. Mim's knees shook as she walked onto the mat.

"Prepare to die!" bellowed June, and Mim's world turned upside down. The first event was over. June had won.

"Fifty-yard dash!" announced Coach Beeker, and Mim,
who was happy to be alive, ran faster than she ever had before.

The second event was over. Mim had won.

Now it was time for the obstacle course.

"For this last event you'll need a partner," said Coach Beeker. While Mim was running a victory lap and June was flexing her muscles, the second and third-graders paired off. Now everybody had a partner except for Mim and June.

Mim and June sat on the bench, sulking.

"I could have won," growled June.

"Me too," whispered Mim.

June looked at Mim. "Well, you are the fastest," she admitted.

Mim looked at June. "And you're the strongest," she said.

"We'd make good partners," said June, and Mim agreed.

Working together, Mim and June were the first-est in the obstacle course.

And then, because it felt right, they were first-est together all the way back to their classrooms.